Good Luck, Mrs. K.!

written by
LOUISE BORDEN

illustrated by
ADAM GUSTAVSON

ALADDIN PAPERBACKS
New York London Toronto Sydney Singapore

First Aladdin Paperbacks edition July 2002
Text copyright © 1999 by Louise Borden
Illustrations copyright © 1999 by Adam Gustavson

ALADDIN PAPERBACKS
An imprint of Simon & Schuster
Children's Publishing Division
1230 Avenue of the Americas
New York, NY 10020

Also available in a Margaret K. McElderry Books hardcover edition.
Designed by Ann Bobco

The text of this book was set in Berkeley Oldstyle ITC.
Printed in Hong Kong
2 4 6 8 10 9 7 5 3 1

The Library of Congress has cataloged the hardcover edition as follows:
Borden, Louise
Good luck, Mrs.K.! / written by Louise Borden ; illustrated by Adam Gustavson.—1st edition.
p.   cm.
Summary: All the students in the third grade are affected when their beloved teacher,
Mrs. Kempczinski is suddenly hospitalized with cancer.
ISBN 0-689-82147-6 (hc)
[1. Teachers—Fiction. 2.Cancer—Fiction. 3. Schools—Fiction.]
I. Gustavson, Adam, ill. II. Title.
PZ7.B64827Gr 1999 [E]—dc21   97-50553
ISBN 0-689-85119-7 (pbk)

91433

In memory of Ann Kempczinski,
for her students and friends at Terrace Park School
and
to celebrate the teaching and classrooms of

Shelley Harwayne
M. K. Kroeger
Terri Pytlik
Ann Sefcovic
Jean McLear
Regie Routman
Franki Sibberson
Karen Szymusiak
Carol Homon
Betty Goerss
Karen Martin
Linda Dodd
Opal Young
Betsy Glick

—L. B.

For H. A. and his cronies

—A. G.

"Say it like this . . . KEMP-CHIN-SKI!"
Mrs. Kempczinski told our class
on the first day of school.
She pointed to her name, written on the blackboard.
"Or you can call me Mrs. K."
I couldn't wait to learn how to spell *Kempczinski*
because I loved the sound of my teacher's name.

That first morning in third grade,
I practiced saying Mrs. Kempczinski's name.

Kemp-chin-ski!

Kemp-chin-ski!

Kemp-chin-ski!

Later, at recess, I played basketball
and said her name another dozen times:

Kemp-chin-ski! Kemp-chin-ski!

Kemp-chin-ski! *Kemp-chin-ski!* *Kemp-chin-ski!*

Kemp-chin-ski! *Kemp-chin-ski!* *Kemp-chin-ski!*

Kemp-chin-ski!

Kemp-chin-ski! *Kemp-chin-ski!* *Kemp-chin-ski!*

I could bounce, dribble, turn, and shoot to that long, fun name.
Twelve shots in a row! *Swish* through the hoop!
Kemp-chin-ski!
It was my own special way to play the game.

Mrs. K. knew *our* names right away . . .
she never mixed them up from the first day of school on.
"I know how it feels when people get your name wrong,"
Mrs. K. said.
"Names are special . . . so take good care of your name."

After that, I liked my own name:
Ann Zesterman.
The capital *A* looked good on my papers, pencil-sharp,
and the *Z* was a big zigzag that was fun to write.
But I still thought *Kempczinski* was the perfect name
for shooting hoops.

And it was the first word on our spelling test that week.
"Say it like this . . . Kemp-chin-ski!" I said to myself
when I wrote out *Kempczinski* at the top of my page.
I liked how the *Z* came right after the *C*.

Mrs. K. had been to faraway places
where no one in third grade had been . . .
cities like London and Rio and even Beijing.
She pinned pictures and maps of the whole world
on the walls of Room 3.
Then she told us she would take us to all those places,
through books.

Sometimes Mrs. Kempczinski called us third-grade explorers.

Or third-grade detectives.

Or third-grade travelers.

When Mrs. K. let me take Olga, the class guinea pig,

out of her cage and hold her in my hands,

I figured third grade was going to be my best grade yet.

Mrs. Kempczinski's two favorite sayings were:
"Be good listeners"
and "Remember to read, read, read."
And Mrs. K. knew sign language
and taught us all some words.
Every recess
she lined us up in silence,
first the girls, then the boys.
On Fridays,
we could bring our skates and RollerBlades for recess,
if we'd done our homework on time.

Every day,
Mrs. K. wore a jangle of keys
that hung on her belt.
In the lunch line,
David Perez and I counted them,
one at a time.
"Thirteen . . . that's a baker's dozen!" said Mrs. K.

In Room 3,
there were more things to learn than a baker's dozen:
all the states and their capitals . . .
how to multiply and divide . . .
a zillion facts about planets and penguins,
poems and worms.
All along, we were still third-grade explorers.
Or third-grade astronauts.
Or third-grade poets or third-grade scientists.
Mrs. K. told us we were all teachers, too.
Every student in our class.
"This year I want you to teach me
what *you* know."
That's what Mrs. Kempczinski told us.
I'd never been called a teacher before,
only a student.

Mrs. Kempczinski always wrote on the blackboard
in her good cursive writing:

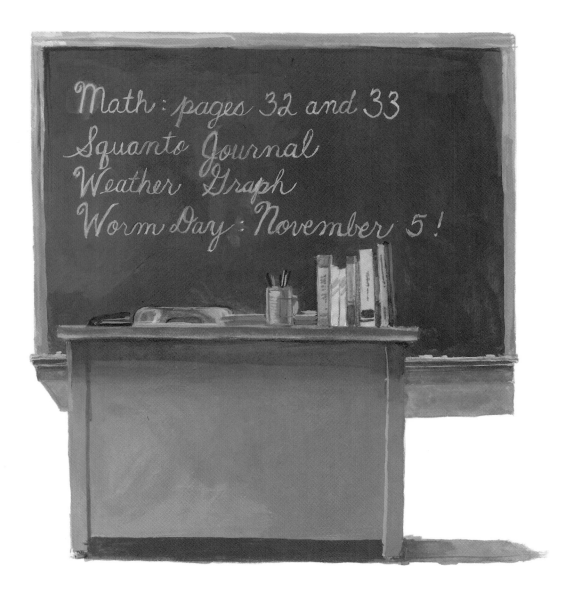

Math: pages 32 and 33
Squanto Journal
Weather Graph
Worm Day: November 5!

Worm Day!
In Room 3,
every day was different, and every day was fun.
All week, we read a stack of books about worms.

Then on Friday we made posters
with important worm facts
and hung them on the walls.
Mrs. K. took real worms
from a big carton of earth
and put one on every desk.
Then she gave us each a hand lens
to study those worms.
That day we were third-grade scientists.
We named our worms and wrote about them.

Mrs. K. even wore plastic worm earrings
to celebrate our Worm Day.

"It's the third-grade way," said Mrs. K.
as we munched on candy worms she gave us for our snack.

Mrs. K. was the tallest teacher in our school.
When Ruthie Elliott asked her how she got to be so tall,
Mrs. K. said, "When all the homework comes in on time,
I do my homework dance
and I grow taller."

"What's a homework dance?"
"I've never seen a teacher dance!"
"Mrs. K. says she knows a special dance!"

So everyone in Room 3 did their homework on time.
Even John Biggs.
Mrs. K. had more than one homework dance . . .
the Cha-cha . . .
the Long Division Dance . . .
the Sword Dance . . .
the Mexican Hat Dance . . .
and the Kempczinski Fan Dance.
We clapped for every one,
but we never saw Mrs. K. grow taller.
"It's the third-grade way,"
Mrs. K. told the second graders next door
when they heard all our noise.

Then we had a substitute teacher for Mrs. K.
For a whole week. Then another week.
Emily Quinn said it was because our teacher had the flu.
Those were the days I said her name at recess,
a baker's dozen times . . .

Kemp-chin-ski!   *Kemp-chin-ski!*   *Kemp-chin-ski!*

Kemp-chin-ski!   *Kemp-chin-ski!*   *Kemp-chin-ski!*

Kemp-chin-ski!   *Kemp-chin-ski!*   *Kemp-chin-ski!*

Kemp-chin-ski!

Kemp-chin-ski!   *Kemp-chin-ski!*   *Kemp-chin-ski!*

I loved to say that name.
I loved the sound of my teacher's name.
Bounce, dribble, turn, and shoot.
Swish through the hoop!

I tried to be a good listener
when Mr. Rivers, the principal,
told us Mrs. K. was in the hospital.
I didn't know how to spell *cancer*
until he wrote it on the board.
I was glad that cancer started with a *C*
instead of that big wonderful *K*
that began my teacher's name.
I pretended Mrs. K. was off to another faraway place . . .
that she was being a third-grade traveler.

Everyone in Room 3 made cards and wrote notes.

Everyone in Room 3 remembered to read, read, read.

It was as if we were reading those stories just for Mrs. K.

Then Mrs. K. wrote us back,

and signed her letter in her own special style:

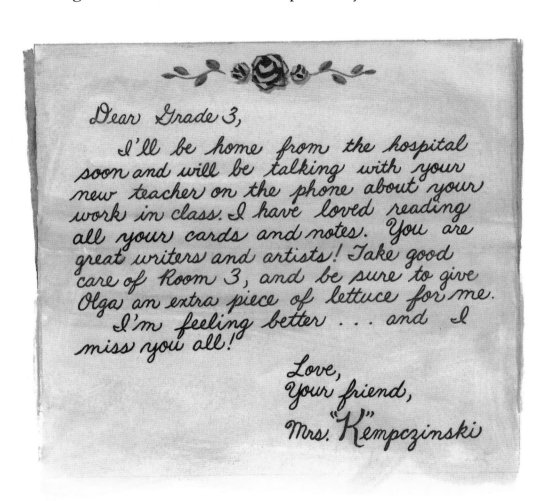

Dear Grade 3,

I'll be home from the hospital soon and will be talking with your new teacher on the phone about your work in class. I have loved reading all your cards and notes. You are great writers and artists! Take good care of Room 3, and be sure to give Olga an extra piece of lettuce for me.

I'm feeling better . . . and I miss you all!

Love,
Your friend,
Mrs. "K"empczinski

Our substitute teacher, Mrs. Dodd,
didn't know any homework dances,
but she knew our names right away,
just like Mrs. K.
At recess,
A. J. Cohen, Eve Smith, and I
taught Mrs. Dodd sign language.
It was fun being the teachers of Room 3.
I gave Mrs. Dodd a thumbs-up sign
when she sank a basket from twelve feet out.
Swish!
She was an *A* student in basketball too,
just like me.

We tried to be good listeners
the day Mr. Rivers said Mrs. K.
had to have another operation.
"How many operations does it take to cure cancer?"
A. J. wanted to know.
Mr. Rivers shook his head and said
there are some answers even principals don't know.

On the first day of May,

Mrs. Dodd helped Room 3 write down the whole year.

Some of us wrote about being third-grade explorers . . .

or scientists . . .

or travelers . . .

or poets . . . or teachers . . .

or readers and writers.

I wrote down that I liked learning to spell

Mrs. Kempczinski's long, fun name,

and that saying *Kemp-chin-ski!* when I played basketball

brought me good shooting luck.

A. J. wrote that Worm Day

was his very favorite day in third grade.

Ted wrote about penguins,

and Emily Quinn said she liked learning about stars

and constellations,

especially the Big Dipper.

Everyone in the class had a best part to share

about being a student in Room 3.

Then Mrs. Dodd stapled all our pages together

and made a book to send to Mrs. K.

Ruthie Elliott said it was the third-grade way.

In early June,
Mr. Rivers asked our whole class to come back
the day after school was out for the summer.

"Bring your roller skates and RollerBlades," he said,
"and Mrs. Dodd and I will have a surprise to celebrate
your hard work this year."

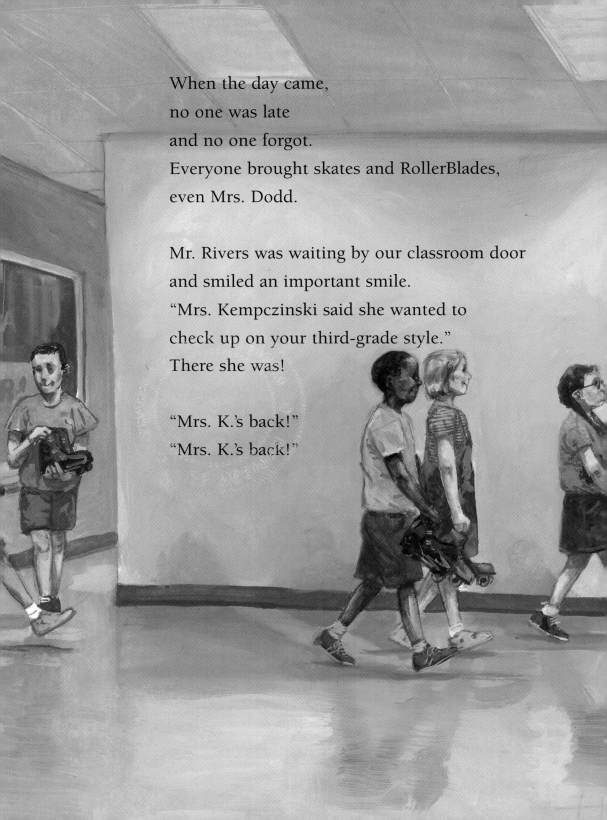

When the day came,
no one was late
and no one forgot.
Everyone brought skates and RollerBlades,
even Mrs. Dodd.

Mr. Rivers was waiting by our classroom door
and smiled an important smile.
"Mrs. Kempczinski said she wanted to
check up on your third-grade style."
There she was!

"Mrs. K.'s back!"
"Mrs. K.'s back!"

I tried to be a good listener
to everyone's questions and to Mrs. K.'s words:
"I hope to be back next fall,
right here in Room 3.
Mainly, I came today to say
you're all terrific!
And I'm proud of your third-grade work."
Mrs. Kempczinski's cheeks weren't as chubby as before,
but I could still hear all that fun
in Mrs. K.'s voice.

Then Mr. Rivers made A. J. the line leader,
the best job of all.
He lined us up in silence,
first the girls,
then the boys.
The whole school
was empty,
waiting for our noise.

One by one,
we skated into the hall,
saying, "GOOD LUCK!" to Mrs. K.
One by one,
we sang her name.
It was the third-grade way.

Kemp-chin-ski!   *Kemp-chin-ski!*   *Kemp-chin-ski!*

Kemp-chin-ski!   *Kemp-chin-ski!*   *Kemp-chin-ski!*

Kemp-chin-ski!

Kemp-chin-ski!   *Kemp-chin-ski!*   *Kemp-chin-ski!*

And she *did* come back in the fall.